IS LOVE A MYSTERY?

ARUN RAJ

This book is dedicated to love because love is a world where there is no caste. Only love is such a means by which we can achieve victory in the world.

Contents

FOREWORD

This book is dedicated to love.Because love is a world where there is no caste.

Only love is such a means,Through which we can achieve victory in the world.

Here the author has shown three scenes, which proves thisHow love has shown love to be paramount.

A new dimension of love is displayed in every story.In the third scene, a girl for whom love was an enemy.

While she was studying, she fell in love, and she loved her love and education.

They take both equally.And in this way different visions of love are found in every scene.

PREFACE

*Every relationship begins when two people
communicate.
Having healthy communication is important
for sharing problems
and find solutions for them. In the absence of
communication,
Relationships fail because of mistrust and
doubt. other thing,
Trust is the foundation of any relationship.
Every relationship starting with family or
friends,
If trust is nil, the relationship is bound to end or
fall.
love is a shared feeling between two people
their interest in each other.
It's not about jealousy, conflict, trial,
Instead love is a positive emotion.
It is the total surrender of your heart to another
person
when you believe that
They will treat your heart better than you.
When someone expresses a lot of love,
You often don't understand how to respond or
express gratitude to him.
The ability to find true love comes from giving
or sharing love.
You can focus more on you based on your
experience
Understand that love is not just a feeling, it is*

your eternal existence,
No matter how much love is expressed in any form, you find yourself in it.
People often love their ideas about something and that's very natural.
When we love someone we care about, we talk well about them, we make sure we don't hurt them.
We feel connected, attached, and emotionally validated while being with them.
They make us feel good about ourselves and we try to do the same,
We also try to keep them feeling good.
Love can make the world a better place to live in.
Only love can win the battle of socio-economic division in the society and nothing else.
The injustice prevailing in the society cannot be removed by anything other than love.
Mother Teresa also used to say the power of love,
Love can make you do miracles in love,
And one should always love the idea of love.
It will make the world a better, happier place to live.

PROLOGUE

People frequently fall in love at first sight.
Then, as time goes on, it fades, gets polluted,
    and vanishes, becoming hatred.
When the same love tree is created, where knowledge has been placed as fertiliser,
    it takes on the characteristics of ancient love and continues to exist through successive births.
We are mindful of it.
The current body, name, form, and relationships do not define you.
You might not be aware of your history or antiquity, but simply being aware of your age is sufficient.Even after starting a relationship, many females' habits alter.
Some people get emotional, while others are intelligent.
Two persons who are in love have a common interest in one another.
Love is a good sensation; it has nothing to do with enmity, strife, or testing.

When you are completely certain that someone else will treat your heart better than you will, you are completely giving your heart over to them.

When someone shows you a lot of affection, it might be difficult to know how to respond or show your appreciation.
Giving or sharing love is the key to finding true love.
    Many girls change their habits even after getting into a relationship.
While some people are clever, others have strong emotions.

There is a shared interest between two people who are in love.

Love is a positive emotion; it is unrelated to hostility, conflict, or testing.

You entirely give your heart over to someone else when you are confident they will take better care of it than you will.

It might be challenging to know how to react or express your gratitude when someone lavishes you with affection.

The secret to discovering true love is to give or share affection.

Acknowledgements

*People frequently fall in love at first sight.
Then, as time goes on, it fades, gets polluted, and
vanishes, becoming hatred.
When the same love tree is created, where
knowledge has been placed as fertiliser, it takes
on the characteristics of ancient love and
continues to exist through successive births.
We are mindful of it.
The current body, name, form, and relationships
do not define you.
You might not be aware of your history or
antiquity, but simply being aware of your age is
sufficient.*

*My buddy Vijay Kumar, Narayan, and K. Priya
are all very appreciated for their tale
recommendations.*

A photo of author Arun Raj giving a speech in public.

I

Mystery?

It is said that no one knows when the time will be kind, it is about those days when Ramesh took leave from his college and joined the reunion of friends, tell that Ramesh is a professor in Geet Bhati and when old friends meet, the past I laugh at those things which used to be serious in those days and slowly everyone started laughing at Ramesh ji and started asking if you talk about the secrets of your two wives, then you listen to those days when my The spirit of doing something was in my mind and I believed research to be everything and in the craze for this research, I came across a sophistication which was very unique i.e. unique,One day,

when May got bored doing research, he came to know about tea poine and took a bike and then I saw something like this, that May forgot himself and started moving forward and continued till he got closer to me. The feeling continued and as soon as May tried to shake hands, she disappeared. Actually, it is about those days when I used to come out of work after night and I saw a beautiful girl sitting there talking about something. I stared at him while riding his bike.

During May, I was attracted to it like a deer running through the woods in search of musk, and all kinds of good and bad thoughts came to my mind. May wanted to talk to him.I started trying and slowly we started talking. And then we started meeting at the same time every day and slowly we fell in love with him. I didn't even know that the one we love was a demonic spirit.

I don't like to call him the devil because he also fell in love with me as much as I did, one day both of us were sitting and a Christian man came out and turned on the bike light and then he started chanting. When my girlfriend started to suffer, then the person imprisoned her, even after six years she could not make her her own and it took me 4 years to forget her and slowly we moved forward in our life.

And he was thinking in his mind that I might be a policeman and he went away, I remember he once mentioned to me about the nearby well that he was in love with a Christian young man when he was young. It was because the Christian young man was attractive to see, slowly our love started growing and one day when I saw that young man doing all those things with another girl, which I would not allow him to do,And we got married.

and sat down with my wife at the same place where we were sitting with her and by chance I saw the man again and he turned off the light,And he was thinking in his mind that I might be a policeman and he went away, I remember he once mentioned to me about the nearby well that he was in love with a Christian young man when he was young. It was because the Christian young man was attractive to see, slowly our love started growing and one day when I saw that young man doing all those things with another girl, which I would not allow him to do,And in this way my way got separated from her and when I asked her again, she said that the young man knew Tantra Vidya and he knew what magic he did that I am not in this world and he imprisoned my soul and he Also gave way that how I will be able to go back to my body, she could say more than me that she was imprisoned and then I told these simple things to my wife, then we thought to help that good soul and then, May started researching about it and I came to know that the solution to *that problem has been found.*

It is said that bad man cannot do anything when God helps, and then on the full moon night such a leela of God happened that the girl got her divine body and married that boy and she should be happy. Felt with both his wives. God punishes every bad person in this world, even if it is late, so by trusting in God, solve every problem as an opportunity of success, Lord ji will remove all the troubles, this is the story of Ramesh ji, who will solve that moment. Feeling close, maybe even today bad people enter the life of good people and try to spoil the life of good person, if you do any work by trusting in God, then its solution is definitely found.

II

Girl started falling in love.

girl for whom love was unsuitable.

when she was studying.

Then what happened was that that girl started falling in love.

Here is the story of two students at IIMT University.

The story is of two such birds who wanted to fly in the sky of love.

It was back in those days when Sanjeev went to enrol in college for the first time.

He was filling out his college form when a voice was heard coming from the side.

Hi, you have an extra pen.

As Sanjeev looked back, he could not mind. Leaving his form, he gave the pen and started looking at it. After seeing that girl, the picture of the girl was deleted from his mind, as if she was looking like that divine afsara that any boy would sacrifice his whole life for that opulent nymph.

And thus, Sanjeev started dreaming of his dreams and

By chance, when he reached the class, he was stunned in his class after seeing him.

He sat down beside her, and they talked softly to each other.

And then Sanjeev was looking for an excuse to talk every day, and slowly he started falling in love.

And it was a matter of the fresher's party, and Sanjeev was waiting to see if he got the task of proposing.

And he called Tanya and proposed on stage, and Tanya didn't mind.

and explained to Sanjeev that I could not do all this.

We can only be good friends. Sanjeev was about to give up hope that Kavya was Sanjeev's best friend.

Kavya's friend Kavya had an unpleasant incident happen with Sanjeev's friend Kavya, due to which Tanya had to stay with Kavya to take care of Kavya. Tanya was one of their roommates.

But an accident happened with Kavya, so Tanya took care of Kavya.

And Kavya Sanjeev and I used to talk for hours. Sanjeev used to tell Kavya everything about his heart. One day, Kavya fell asleep.

During the call, Sanjeev shared his heart with Kavya.

And she was Tanya on the call. After all, Tanya had not talked to Sanjeev for 6 months.

And then, when Tanya understood that Sanjeev is a good boy and there is no harm in being friends with Sanjeev, one day, Sanjeev told Tanya about his heartache, and Tanya came to Sanjeev's talk.

And a new story started. In this way, Sanjeev awakened love in Tanya's heart.

And, fleeing the sight of the world and the hunters, these birds took to the new sky.

But where was this love going to look good at the time?

Tanyal and Sanjeev began to live solely for each other as time passed.

His love was not even for the body; his love was like a bird soaked in it.

Who knew that we had to prove ourselves in the world and get love?

Tanya was eventually hired by a multinational corporation.

Sanjeev went to Dubai after three years when Sanjeev came

By then, Tanya was about to get engaged, and Tanya told the family members.

They agreed, and both of them got married.

But after two years of marriage, Sanjeev gets attracted to a girl.

At six, to get him, he started ignoring Tanya.

And as Tanya started to grow closer to her, the matter kept getting away from her.

Gone are the days when Anamika and Sanjeev used to work in the same office.

And working till late at night, Sanjeev got a chance.

I have got to leave the house. Sanjeev fulfils the desires of his heart.

He wanted the ghost who was riding on him to express his wish.

Anamika was an open-hearted girl. She also agreed.

But that day, Sanjeev was feeling guilty in Anamika's sari.

Her sleeveless blouse was blowing her senses as she walked.

He proceeded, but he stopped and refused to first divorce his wife.

Take it. It is said that no desire can make anyone a criminal.

Anamika, the love that had been loved for years, left.

He did all that a wife does to give happiness to her husband, Sanjeev, too.

He was happy because, after finding Anamika, he had gone to heaven slowly.

The game went on, but Anamika loved David's money.

David was the boss of the company, and Anamika worked for David.

Sanjeev left Sanjeev and said, "Good and bad," but then Sanjeev realised

He again brought Tanya to mind and apologized.

Then they did not even think of making a mistake. Now Sanjeev Tanya also has two children.

and living life happily.

III

Evils of girls

Sometimes it happens in our life that our heart unwillingly pushes us into that quagmire from where it becomes difficult to get out, it is a matter of those days when we i.e. Rajiv was doing MBA from an engineering college in Maharashtra, We had passed a year in Corona and we were 5 boys in a batch of 20 children, and we did not talk to any girl nor did we want to do it, because we knew what raita was spread among the girls ,

as soon as a year passed we all started going to college and slowly a girl Kavya who was the best looking girl in the class started coming closer to me, meaning I started to forcefully envolve in my gossips and in many things close to us Slowly the time kept on coming and we stayed as Sanyasi Baba means the one who knew all the evils of girls and was spreading raita inside.

Sometimes I feel that why the next person is praising so much, but every boy likes it, we also used to listen silently, one day some talk happened that he started saying that people think something opposite about our relationship. We were saint men, we explained it well, and Kavya often used to give street messages to the boys who used to message her and one day we came to know that she is hanging out with another boy, about whom she used to say the opposite,

and After a few months, I came to know that Kavya was also preaching about me in reverse and slowly all my friends came together to learn the right lesson from Kavya and Kavya's art sheet came in front of everyone and she ran away from amongst us. As if someone is getting rid of an old worm,
Lessons are learned from such an incident that keep a proper distance from the girl and achieve your objective, this is what Rajiv ji did and today he is doing PhD from IIM, a good institute of India.

॰

ARUN RAJ

IV
Symbol of love

It is said that 40 years ago, on the forest side of Sheikhpur Gram Panchayat in Amarodha block of Kanpur Dehat (present day), there was a large village of Yadavas on the forest side of Sheikhpur Gram Panchayat, which the British used to call Malhe Pur State. The village is adjacent, says the head of Basavan Pur. The village of Ki Malhe Pur dates back to the Mughal era. The Yadavs, who lived in the Mughal Sultanate, were desolate and fighters. There is a famous story. An English officer once visited the village. And he asked the villager to take him on the path that leads from the village to the forest side. On this, he pointed out which side of the road he was pointing his feet. On which the British went. But he asked Patwari,who were these people? Patwari said, "These people are very dangerous." So the British officer said. After all, who is this?

So Patwari said, "The government ,he is Yadav."
So the British officer said, "These people will
not come into easy control." Patwari spoke only
when he had to think about something. The
government can control it only two days a year.
A Holi and a Diwali. And then a new story
begins here. The English officer's daughter used
to visit the forest. And she used to take a bath
in the well of the village. And this was often the
case. -- One day, a young man in the village was
taking a bath. And Lily, the English officer's girl,
saw him taking a bath. So she could not stop
herself and she started loving him. After a few
days, he also liked her and her dressing sense.

Slowly, that young man also fell in love with
Lily, and I forgot that Lily was a British officer's
girl. And such a deep love for the girl was
scorched in the fire. They had forgotten
everything in love of both.It was a matter of
one day that Lily was taking a shower. And
the raghu, a young man, came. And often, Lily
and Raghu roamed together in the forest. After a
few months, they met and fell in love with each
other. They started a new life together and both
got married according to Hindu custom.

A British officer came to her daughter and said
to go. She had given him away. The British office
started thinking of taking revenge on the raghu.
And then Patwari said that on Holi and Diwali,

these people drink a lot of alcohol. If you attack in the morning on that day, they can come under control. Gradually, the time for Diwali has come, the British fire in that village. Due to being set on fire, the whole village was set on fire. And the British committed a great massacre. And during that time, English lilies and raghu were killed. And the singers immortalised their love. He started worshipping that as a symbol of love.

V
Untold tales of Love and Affection

And thus slowly my first semester was
over,
And then comes the second semester
when I and my friends opened up ,

and did a variety of adventures.
Like going to the hostel's boundary to
go to drink tea ,

and just Satania started and Makkari
made it home ,

and we started going to college work because,

he was good at reading and even the teacher doesn't say much.
I believe that if there is one quality, 10 evil hides.

And was about to finish my first year that a fresher party took place ,

and I had to propose to a girl. I made a friend who looked good.
One thing happens if the girl rejects you,

then the status of respect would be in engineering.

But this did not happen to me and that girl did not auction my honor.

Then what was left.

I accounted for the girl the other day,

and my life was getting over by the end
of such years.

ॐ

that was the time when a boy fall in
love ....

when i am in 8th class ,i like girl.she is
very precious to me bcz of her nature
....

i am fall in love with her but i am
affraid to show my love with her......

when your childhood friend know that
you have fall in love with girl ,

they tease you with her name ....

When I met her in class ....I felt good
that day........

In the age of 13/15th, you meet the girl who was different from others....

you really like her........

Now my one sided Love was started........as soon as we grewup.....

.we become close friend on 9th class with help of my best friend ......

When we join highschool.......we both are topper of our sections........

.there was one thing to notice that we both are competitive for each other......as soon as Time extended.....

We were too close to each other......and my first and last love begun.........

After the precious time I know that the first love is incredible to HEART.

ॐ

Often we talk of love.
So we reach our childhood.
Everyone has a loving friend in their life.
My one-sided story of love also finally started.
My love really started when we were studying in eighth grade.
We often quarreled with friends to sit with him.
Actually his section used to be just in front of our section.
Whenever he was able to go to his class,
So the heart was very relaxed.
Slow love started unilaterally and we knew when we grew up selling these childish antics.
And our life has got new experiences and meanings.
And our unilateral love could not be reconciled.
MY LOVE wandered from one section to another and died.

જી

Let us talk about the narrow view of the present youth, by looking at love, its meaning has been reduced and it has been limited to love.

It can be said that it would be wrong to call only attraction ,

as love because both attraction and love are different.

Difference between the two is different,

then attraction can change according to the circumstances and location,

but it does not happen in love.

A big question currently arises among the youth is whether both education and *love are possible together, how much they have an effect on each other and how it can determine the direction and condition of a person's life is a very funny thing.*

That everyone sees love from a different perspective.

And in that context, the definitions of love are changed even if both studies and love are complementary to each other or are opposite to each other or both have nothing to do with each other or not,

it is quite complicated because it depends on the person His perspective on nature and his views on nature.

Many examples can be seen around us in which a person says that I have been inhabited by love,

then someone says ruined. Just think why this is love,

is it really capable of ruining or inhabiting a person,

then yes It can be said that it is capable but it does not love it ,

all depends on the attitude of the person who loves,

if a person loves someone without any selfishness then of course love should never betray him or never ruin him.

Will do and if a person pretends love for selfishness or

if he gives the name of attraction to love,

then it can also go towards waste.

Love between two people is a shared feeling about

their interest in one another.

It is not about jealousy, conflict, testing,

instead love is a positive feeling.

It is the total surrender of your heart to another person

when you have that confidence that

they will treat your heart better than you will.

When someone expresses a lot of love,

you often do not understand how to react or express gratitude to him.

The ability to find true love comes from giving or sharing of love.

he more focused you are, on the basis of your experience you can

understand that love is not just an emotion, it is your eternal existence.

no matter how much love is expressed in any form, you find yourself in it.

people are often in love with their ideas of something and that is very natural.

ೞ

The matter is of those six months ago when we used to go to the court to play basketball and during the same time when we used to play in the tennis court also sometimes,

one day we saw a strange face and that girl was in a sports cap and table tennis Was playing and then the look of her gentle face does not take its name, then the day-to-day work was done playing, and then slowly her eyes turned towards the eyes and if you do not look for a day, then the heart Began to be restless, and once again started looking for his number or place to talk and one day got her id on instagram and then sent request and send cancel attitude lasted for 6 months because he didn't accept the request, one day I see The key request was accepted and the follow request also came from there and then we slowly started talking and now we have become very good friends.

VI

A Married life

Even the wordless exchange between them that he had preserved from the past ended the day after that. She could see the pain and resentment written on his face, but for how long could she hide from his prying eyes by disguising herself as someone else? He had given up hoping for Arun to say something. She is unsure of what is inside them. Why does he cast his own flames of fire upon it? His stillness interferes with my own fulfilment. Call it the start of the tale or the pinnacle of happiness...

She had her younger brother Parash, a Trisha student, with her when Arun had visited her. Because of their close connection, it was arranged that, under any circumstances, whomever loses the debating match will make the winner flawless in any one subject. Although the transaction was enjoyable, Trisha frequently avoided hard work in favour of leisurely employment. The event was about to begin. Parash's expression was filled with fear, but Trisha's was devoid of fear. Parash entered the stage and lost due to his "Sh."

He would speak when he needed to do so effectively. Sunita to sunita and vegetarian to vegetarian By correctly utilising the phrases, satisfaction won the competition.According to the terms of the contract, Trisha wanted to study arithmetic, and impoverished Parash patiently taught Trisha how to calculate HCF, speed, distance, and time, as well as percentages. A space in the heart was made for Parash as a result of this ongoing relationship. He occasionally sat on the dupatta of someone and, as he pulled it, his shoulders began to rub against each other. Parash would then get up and pick up the man's dupatta. Small details were crucial for satisfaction, yet Parash was amusing, flippant, and cunning. He was unconcerned with all of these issues.

He refused to read Mills and Boons books or watch love movies. He would have had news articles, periodicals, and debates about both domestic and foreign affairs. Parash would tell Trisha things related to politics and Trisha would tell him stories from romantic novels.Arun's connection developed throughout the course of the following several days, albeit this lovely companionship may have assumed the shape of love. Family members of Arun immediately took to Trisha. She was made the daughter-in-law of that home in less than a month. The nature of arun and contentment varies significantly. Arun was stern and impatient, in contrast to Trisha's joy and playfulness. He had demonstrated his resentment from the first night on.

Trisha waited for him in her room. He was about to fall asleep when arun entered the room carrying a foul odour. As soon as he got there, he collapsed face down on the bed and quickly fell asleep. Uncertain of what hour of the night Arun began groping Trisha. He had the impression that his body contained thousands of scorpions. Even though she was perspiring, she managed to hold her scream in by placing both palms over her lips. Arun slept off once again, but Trisha continued thinking, "Does a guy not know how to share happiness?" He wants to grasp everything, but why? Is it only that he knows how to grab it?If this is the happiness of married life, then perhaps she will not be able to maintain this marriage. That fateful night after the wedding passed with great difficulty.